Contents

What do firefighters do?   4

Things to make and do
Dress like a firefighter   6

The fire engine   8

Putting out the fire   10

At the fire station   12

Play the part
Emergency, car on fire!   14

Flash flood   16

Smoke alarm drama   18

Hurry, it's the fire alarm!   20

Hurry, it's the fire alarm! (continued)   22

Glossary   24

Index   24

What do firefighters do?

Firefighters work for the **Fire and Rescue Service**. They put out fires and rescue people from blazes. Firefighters help in other kinds of emergencies, too. They are called out to car accidents, floods, building collapses, chemical spills and will even rescue trapped animals!

FIREFIGHTER

Written by Liz Gogerly

Photographs by Chris Fairclough

WAYLAND

Published in 2014 by Wayland

Copyright © Wayland 2014

Wayland
338 Euston Road
London NW1 3BH

Wayland Australia
Level 17/207 Kent Street
Sydney, NSW 2000

Editors: Paul Humphrey, James Nixon
Design: Rob Norridge and D. R. ink
Commissioned photography: Chris Fairclough
Model maker: Tom Humphrey

Picture credits: South Wales Fire and Rescue Service: p. 7 top;
West Midlands Fire Service Photogrpahic: pp. 4, 5, 10 bottom.
British Library Cataloguing in Publication Data
Gogerly, Liz.
Firefighter -- (Play the part)
1. Fire fighters--Juvenile literature. 2. Fire fighters--
Juvenile drama. 3. Role playing--Juvenile literature.
I. Title II. Series
363.3'78-dc22

ISBN 978 0 7502 8872 9

First published in 2011 by Wayland

Printed in China

Wayland is a division of Hachette Children's Books,
an Hachette UK Company

www.hachette.co.uk

The author, packager and publisher
would like to thank Davigdor Infants'
School, Hove for their help and
participation in this book.

A firefighter's job is all about saving lives and protecting everyone from danger. It can be risky, but it's a very exciting job.

Firefighters climb ladders to put out fires and rescue people from the tops of buildings.

Dress like a firefighter

When an emergency call comes through firefighters quickly put on their **protective** fire kit. Fire kit is **fire-resistant** and **waterproof**. Firefighters also wear a yellow helmet with a **visor** to protect their eyes.

Firefighters spend a lot of their working day at the fire station. There, they wear stationwear. This is usually grey trousers and a light-coloured shirt.

visor

radio

torch

protective fire kit

When firefighters go into a place where there is smoke they wear **breathing apparatus**.

breathing apparatus

There are lots of different firefighter costumes available that you could buy. These can look like real fire kit and will turn you into a firefighter ready for action! Some shops also have firefighter cases which come with **sirens**, axes and **fire extinguishers**.

The fire engine

The fire engine is used to carry firefighters to the scene of an emergency. Fire can quickly cause damage and endanger people's lives so fire engines need to move fast. Blue flashing lights and loud sirens warn people that a fire engine needs to pass quickly.

Make your own fire engine

1. Cut the top and bottom flaps off a large cardboard box and paint it red.

2. To make the front window, draw a large rectangle on the front of the box at the top. Paint the window white.

3. To make the lights, draw a circle on each side of the front of the box at the bottom. Paint the circles white.

You will need:

★ Large rectangular cardboard box
★ Red, yellow, black and white paint
★ 4 paper plates
★ Glue

4 To make the radiator grill, draw a long rectangle shape between the lights. Paint it black.

5 Draw a long thin strip along each side of the fire engine. Paint it yellow.

6 To make the wheels, take the four paper plates. Paint the edges black, and paint the centre white.

7 Glue the wheels to the bottom of the fire engine.

Get your fire engine ready for action

Stick the plastic hooks to the outside of your fire engine. Neatly coil up the rope and hose and hang them on the hooks. Next arrange equipment, such as plastic axe, buckets and fire extinguisher, on the hooks or hanging off the side of the engine.

You will need:

★ Rope or washing line
★ Plastic garden hose or washing machine hose to use as a fire hose
★ Plastic axe
★ Plastic hammer
★ Buckets
★ Toy fire extinguisher
★ Plastic self-adhesive hooks
★ Sticky tape

Putting out the fire

A fire engine carries fire hoses and **water pumps** to put out fires. Some engines have a water tank to supply the water. Most engines pump water from **fire hydrants**. If there isn't a fire hydrant nearby then they get water from rivers, lakes or even swimming pools!

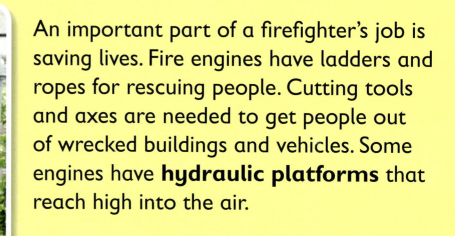

An important part of a firefighter's job is saving lives. Fire engines have ladders and ropes for rescuing people. Cutting tools and axes are needed to get people out of wrecked buildings and vehicles. Some engines have **hydraulic platforms** that reach high into the air.

Make your own fire extinguisher

You will need:
....
★ Empty plastic bottle
★ A plastic clothes peg
★ Thin black card
★ Red and black paint
★ Sticky tape
★ Glue

1. Paint a plastic bottle with red paint apart from the neck of the bottle. When the first coat of paint has dried add another coat of paint.

2. Paint the neck of the bottle with black paint. Add an extra coat of paint when it is dry.

3. Take the thin black card and cut out a rectangle measuring 10 cm by 8 cm.

4. Roll the piece of card to make a small tube. Fasten the ends of the card together with sticky tape.

5. Paint the clothes peg black.

6. Tape one end of the peg into the tube so that the two handles at the other end stick out of the tube.

7. Finally, tape the tube to the top of the bottle to complete the fire extinguisher.

8. In role play you can use your fire extinguisher on brightly coloured 'flames' cut out from tissue paper.

At the fire station

Firefighters wait for emergency calls at the fire station. Firefighters are on duty day and night. Inside most fire stations there are kitchens, bathrooms and rooms for sleeping and relaxing.

There are also offices, fitness rooms and **training** areas at the fire station, too. Many stations have a **drill tower** where the firefighters can practise their rescue skills.

Emergency calls reach the fire station by telephone or radio. Many fire stations have an alarm or siren that goes off. This alerts the firefighters to the emergency and they get ready for action.

Set up a fire station

Place a computer and a phone on top of the table and arrange chairs around the desk. This is where the firefighters relax while they are waiting for emergency calls. You can put cups and food on the table, too. Make sure that the fire engine you made on pages 8–9 is fully equipped for an emergency. Finally, get the fire kit ready for the firefighters to put on.

You will need:

★ A table
★ 2 chairs
★ Phone
★ Computer
★ Paper
★ Toy cups and food
★ Books
★ Fire kit or firefighting costumes
★ The fire engine, equipped and ready to go!

You have set the scene and made some props. Now you can begin to play the part of a firefighter in these role plays.

Emergency, car on fire!

Find out what it's like to be firefighters at the scene of a car crash. You can use a toy pedal car, or an upturned table attached with wheels made from paper plates.

 FIREFIGHTER 1: Oh dear. The car is badly smashed.

 FIREFIGHTER 2: Let's get the driver out quick!

 FIREFIGHTER 1: (*firefighter uses axe to open car*) Don't worry, we're here to help. How are you feeling?

 DRIVER: I am trapped. I can't move.

 FIREFIGHTER 2: (*firefighter helps the driver free*) That should do it…

DRIVER: Thank you so much.

FIREFIGHTER 2: Come on, let's help you into the ambulance.

FIREFIGHTER 1: Oh no! The car's engine is on fire…

WHAT HAPPENS NEXT?

You can decide what happens next in this scene. Below are some fun ideas that you could try acting out using your own words. Then have a go at making up your own scenes.

1 The firefighters tackle the blaze with hoses and fire extinguishers and manage to put it out.

2 The firefighters manage to get well away from the car before it blows up. The driver thanks the firefighters for saving his life.

3 The firefighters get the driver out while the car is on fire. The driver has breathed in lots of smoke and needs an ambulance to take him to hospital.

Flash flood

Sometimes firefighters are called out to rescue people caught in a flood. Play the part of firefighters who rescue a family trapped in their home. You could use a playhouse for the home and a toy inflatable boat as the rescue boat. Use a blue sheet for the floodwater.

FIREFIGHTER 1: (*puts down the telephone*) The river has burst its banks! The High Street is flooded. The Smiths at number 6 are trapped.

FIREFIGHTER 2: (*jumps up from the table where he's been reading a book*) Let's put on our kit, get in the engine and go.

(*The sirens on the fire engine go off as they rush to the flood.*)

MRS SMITH: (*waving from the window of the house*) Help! We're stuck in here.

FIREFIGHTER 1: (*gets out of the fire engine*) The water is very high. We need the rescue boat.

MRS SMITH: Please hurry. My husband has injured himself.

FIREFIGHTER 2: (*firefighters in the rescue boat paddling to the house*) Don't panic, we're on our way.

WHAT HAPPENS NEXT?

You can decide what happens next in this scene. Below are some fun ideas that you could try acting out using your own words. Then have a go at making up your own scenes.

1 The firefighters reach the house in the boat. All the family climb out of the window into the boat.

2 The firefighters struggle against the rising floodwater to reach the house. They need to tie a rope to the house and use it to pull the boat next to the window.

3 The firefighters reach the house. Mr Smith cannot walk so one of the firefighters has to lift him out of the house.

Smoke alarm drama

Play the part of firefighters who rush to help when a smoke alarm goes off at a house.

FIREFIGHTER 1: (*puts down the telephone*) The smoke alarm at the Browns' is going off. They don't know if it's a fire or not.

FIREFIGHTER 2: Better get ready for action.

(*The firefighters put on fire kit, get in the fire engine and go!*)

FIREFIGHTER 1: (*fire engine pulls up at the house and the firefighters jump out*) It's certainly smoky! (*coughs*)

FIREFIGHTER 2: Hello, are you the family that lives here?

MRS BROWN: Yes. We heard the alarm and got out quickly.

MR BROWN: (*looks upset*) Well, not all of us got out… what about Fluffy?

 MRS BROWN: He's our dog!

 FIREFIGHTER 1: Don't panic! We'll find him.

WHAT HAPPENS NEXT?

You can decide what happens next in this scene. Below are some fun ideas that you could try acting out using your own words. Then have a go at making up your own scenes.

1 The fire spreads all over the house. The firefighters fight the fire with hoses and extinguishers. Meanwhile, Fluffy runs up to them – the naughty dog wasn't in the house after all.

2 The firefighters don't find a fire. Instead, they find some burnt toast that has popped out of the toaster. It must have caused the smoke alarm to go off.

3 The firefighters fight a fire in the kitchen. They soon put it out and save Fluffy. The dog is alive but rather wet!

Hurry, it's the fire alarm!

Play the part of firefighters tackling a blaze at a local shop.

FIREFIGHTER 1: (*wakes with a start when the fire alarm goes off at the fire station*) What's happening?

FIREFIGHTER 2: You were having a nap! Quick. Get your fire kit on! The fire alarm at Sam's Store is going off!

(*The firefighters quickly put on their kits and helmets.*)

FIREFIGHTER 2: (*dashes to the fire engine*) I checked all the equipment this morning. Everything's ready.

FIREFIGHTER 1: (*jumps in the fire engine*) I'm ready for action too!

(*The fire engine sirens go off as the firefighters rush to the fire.*)

FIREFIGHTER 1: When these drivers get their cars out of the way we'll be there in no time.

FIREFIGHTER 2: I can see the smoke from here. The fire must be bad.

FIREFIGHTER 1: (*pulls up at Sam's Store*) Let's get the hose down and attach it to the water pump.

SAM: Help! My shop's burning down!

FIREFIGHTER 2: Don't panic Sam. We'll have it under control in no time. Is everyone out of there?

SAM: Well, I think so… The alarm bell went off and everyone ran out.

(continued over page)

Hurry, it's the fire alarm!

(continued)

 FIREFIGHTER 2: Let's get to it! (*pulls down visor and shines a torch inside the shop to see if anyone is trapped*) I can't see anyone. Start the hoses. (*The firefighters begin to squirt water at the fire.*)

 FIREFIGHTER 2: It's not as bad as it looks. It's nearly out.

FIREFIGHTER 1: I'll get the fire extinguishers to finish off.

MRS SINGH: Help!

SAM: That sounded like Mrs Singh – she was shopping when the fire alarm went off.

 FIREFIGHTER 1: Sounded like it came from inside. She must be trapped.

 FIREFIGHTER 2: We better get her out…

Shop

WHAT HAPPENS NEXT?

You can decide what happens next in this scene. Below are some fun ideas that you could try acting out using your own words. Then have a go at making up your own scenes.

1 There is thick smoke everywhere, but the firefighters manage to carry Mrs Singh out of there as quickly as possible.

2 The firefighters go inside the smoky shop. They find Mrs Singh lying under fallen shelves. They manage to cut her out using axes and tools.

3 When the firefighters go into the shop there is an explosion. A box of fireworks goes off and they have to dash out of the shop. Meanwhile, Mrs Singh is already outside having escaped out of the back.

GLOSSARY

breathing apparatus Equipment that helps you breathe.

drill tower A tall building at a fire station, used for training.

Fire and Rescue Service The organisation that responds to emergencies, such as fire, floods and collapsed buildings.

fire extinguisher A metal cylinder containing water or foam for spraying on to a fire.

fire hydrant A pipe in a street from which firefighters can draw water.

fire-resistant Describes something that is protected against fire.

hydraulic platform A moving platform powered by the pressure of a liquid being pushed through a tube.

protective Describes something that stops you from being harmed.

siren A warning device which makes a loud wailing noise.

training Practising the skills for a particular job

visor A see-through shield attached to a helmet which can be pulled down to protect the face and eyes.

water pump A machine used to force water in a particular direction.

waterproof Describes clothing that does not let water through and keeps you dry.

INDEX

accidents 4, 14
axe 7, 9, 10, 14, 23

breathing apparatus 7

emergency calls 6, 13

fire engine 8–9, 10, 13, 16, 17, 18, 20
fire extinguisher 7, 9, 11, 15, 19, 22
fire hydrant 10

fire kit 6–7, 13, 16, 18, 20
fire station 6, 12–13
floods 4, 16–17

helmet 6, 20
hoses 10, 15, 19, 21, 22

radio 6, 13
role play 14–23

sirens 7, 8, 13, 16, 20
smoke 7, 15, 18–19, 21, 23

torch 6, 22
training 12

visor 6, 22

water pump 10, 21